Junkyard Dan

Bloody Knife

NOX PRESS
books for that extra kick to give you more power
www.NoxPress.com

Also by Elise Leonard:

The **JUNKYARD DAN** series: (*Nox Press*)
1. Start of a New Dan
2. Dried Blood
3. Stolen?
4. Gun in the Back
5. Plans
6. Money for Nothing
7. Stuffed Animal
8. Poison, Anyone?
9. A Picture Tells a Thousand Dollars
10. Wrapped Up
11. Finished
12. Bloody Knife
13. Taking Names and Kicking Assets
14. Mercy

THE SMITH BROTHERS (a series): (*Nox Press*)
1. All for One
2. When in Rome
3. Get a Clue
4. The Hard Way
5. Master Plan

A LEEG OF HIS OWN (a series): (*Nox Press*)
1. Croaking Bullfrogs, Hidden Robbers
2. 20,000 LEEGS Under the C
3. Failure to Lunch
4. Hamlette

The **AL'S WORLD** series: (*Simon & Schuster*)
Book 1: Monday Morning Blitz
Book 2: Killer Lunch Lady
Book 3: Scared Stiff
Book 4: Monkey Business

The **LEADER** series: (*Nox Press*)
- ✭ Honor
- ✭ Courage
- ✭ Respect
- ✭ Service
- ✭ Integrity
- ✭ Commitment
- ✭ Loyalty
- ✭ Duty

Junkyard Dan

Bloody Knife

Elise Leonard

NOX PRESS
books for that extra kick to give you more power
www.NoxPress.com

Leonard, Elise
Junkyard Dan series / Bloody Knife
ISBN: 978-1-935366-05-8

Copyright © 2009 by Elise Leonard.
All rights reserved, including the right of reproduction in whole or in part in any form. Published by Nox Press.
www.NoxPress.com

First Nox Press printing: June 2009
Second Nox Press printing: April 2010

books for that extra kick to give you more power

This book is dedicated to Brian James Kenney, the son of Russell J. Kenney, an adult literacy tutor from the Literacy Volunteers of Livingston County, Inc. in Mount Morris, NY.

I know that Karen Six, the Executive Director, purchased a set of the Junkyard Dan books as a memorial to Brian, but I wanted to personally acknowledge Brian and Russell Kenney as well.

I'm honored that the Literacy Volunteers of Livingston County chose my books to help Brian live on in memory, and I humbly applaud their commitment to helping others find a better life through literacy, even during such sad times.

I hope your learners find much success, and I appreciate your praise and thanks, but it is *you*, the many tutors and educators out in the field, working hard to help people obtain literacy who should be praised and thanked.

I'd also like to dedicate this book to Tom Flores from the Ventura County Library Adult Literacy Program in California. I'm *so* glad you are enjoying this series, but please don't forget to PICK UP YOUR WIFE!

And many thanks to Carol Chapman, Paula Petrossi, Deborah Fox and Ann Leffingwell, for sharing our books with everyone. We think you guys rock! ☺

To my readers:
Sometimes, the journey isn't that much fun.
But *some* things are worth that journey.
Obtaining literacy is worth the journey.
Thank you for allowing me
to take that journey with you.

~Elise

Chapter 1

Someone once said, "He who fears something gives it power over him."

Rico feared what was happening to him.

He had reason to fear it.

* * *

I couldn't sleep all night.

I kept tossing and turning.

I was thinking about Rico. And how frustrated he must be.

He said he was framed.

I kept putting myself in his shoes.

I don't know how I'd deal with that.

And I don't know how I'd live with it, either.

If he *had* been framed? I sure hope we could prove it. I also hoped we could find the *real* killer.

The problem? We had to do it *before* Rico got convicted.

And that didn't give us much time.

Everything pointed to him.

We would have to find some solid evidence. You know, to overturn what was already found.

But how?

Where?

I had no clue as to what to do.

I was thinking about that when my phone rang.

"Hello?"

"Hi Dan."

It was Rosa.

I hopped out of bed.

"Where are you?" I asked.

"Headed for the public defender's office. I want to discuss Rico's case with her. Want to come?"

"Do you want me to come?" I asked.

Bloody Knife

"Yes."

"When will you get here?" I asked.

"In about five minutes."

"I'll be ready," I said.

While we were speaking? I was grabbing at clothes.

Pulling them on.

I ran to brush my teeth as soon as I hung up.

I splashed on some after shave.

Then I raced to feed the dogs and cats.

Rosa pulled up as I was feeding the cats.

"Don't worry. Keep going," she said. "I'll wait inside for you."

When I got back in? She was sitting on the couch.

Lucky was curled up next to her.

On the couch.

With his head in her lap.

Like I keep saying. He's a smart dog!

I swear I could see him smiling.

He's no fool.

"Are you hungry? Want some breakfast?" I

asked Rosa.

She shrugged.

"I'm not really hungry. I'm too upset to eat."

I understood that.

This whole thing with Rico? I sort of lost my appetite too.

"How about a fruit and grain bar?" I offered.

Rosa smiled. "Have any with chocolate?"

I looked in my cabinet. I had a variety pack.

It came with strawberry, blueberry and chocolate chip.

"You're in luck," I said.

I grabbed the whole box.

"Want me to make coffee?" I asked.

She shook her head. "I'd rather just go."

I nodded.

"We can stop on the way, if you want to," I offered.

She nodded.

We hopped into my car and drove off.

The public defender's office was in the city. So we had a bit of a drive.

Bloody Knife

We were finally in the city. And I parked the car.

We passed a deli as we walked to the lawyer's office.

"Mind if I stop in and get something to drink?" Rosa asked.

"No problem," I said.

We went in and Rosa got a tiny container of chocolate milk.

I got some regular milk.

We got to the lawyer's office minutes later.

"So what is your defense?" Rosa asked the young lawyer.

"I haven't come up with anything yet," she replied.

"The trial is about to start. Don't you think you *should*?!" Rosa asked.

"Well, the evidence is damaging. But I looked to see if it was processed wrong. So we could get it thrown out."

Rosa looked hopeful.

"Was it processed wrong?" Rosa asked.

"No."

Rosa's shoulders slumped.

"So now what?" I asked.

The lawyer shrugged.

"Look," Rosa told her. "He's not guilty. He didn't do it. I know he *looks* guilty. But he's not."

The young lawyer looked at us.

"If he's not guilty? We're going to have to *prove* it," she said. "And in a perfect world? It would be great if we knew who *did* do it."

"We need to go speak with him," Rosa said.

So we left for the prison.

All three of us.

Chapter 2

We took two cars.

Rosa and I took mine. The young lawyer took her own car.

As we drove there? We were quiet. Somber.

Rosa finally spoke.

"If we don't help Rico? He'll go away for life," Rosa said softly.

"Most likely."

"I can't live with that," she said.

I looked at her.

There was a tear sliding down her cheek.

I reached over. I swept the tear from her cheek.

"I need to solve this," she whispered.

"Okay, Rosa," I said. "We will try. We'll do it

together."

She nodded.

We drove a little further in silence.

Each with our own thoughts.

My thoughts were on Rosa. And how she was such a good person.

She cared about others.

She had a good heart.

She was smart and strong. But she had a soft side.

To me? That was the perfect woman.

Smart and strong. Yet also soft.

Patti was smart and strong. But she wasn't soft.

She wasn't loving.

She didn't care about people as Rosa did.

Patti cared about *things*. But not people.

Rosa was the opposite.

She cared about people. Not things.

I was thinking those thoughts when Rosa spoke.

"You are going to get a glimpse of my dark side," she said.

Bloody Knife

I laughed.

"You *have* a dark side?" I asked.

"Oh yeah," Rosa said. "And it's not pretty."

That made me laugh.

"I can't imagine you having a dark side."

She cracked up.

"Oh come on, Dan. You *must* have heard that Hispanics are hot-headed."

"I don't believe stuff like that," I said. "I don't believe that an entire race can have one trait. That's just silly."

Rosa giggled. "When you put it like that? You sound right."

"I *am* right. It doesn't make sense that an entire race of people are the same."

"Okay. So maybe I am using that as an excuse. But I *am* angry. And I *will* get ugly, if I need to."

I smiled at Rosa.

"Rosa? If Rico *was* framed, we *should* get ugly! I'll get ugly, too!"

Rosa giggled. "You could never get ugly."

"Hey," I said. "I may not be Hispanic. But I can

get ugly."

Then I thought about what I'd just said.

"Wait a minute," I said. "Maybe the word shouldn't be 'ugly.' Maybe the word we should be using is... passionate."

I looked at Rosa.

"I *can* be passionate, you know," I told her. "*Very* passionate."

Then I turned beet red.

Because if anyone or anything could bring out my passionate side? It was Rosa.

I tried not to look at Rosa.

But I *did* sneak a peek.

Her face was as red as mine must have been. She was blushing too.

I was talking about being passionate about an issue. About righting wrongs.

But there was another kind of passion.

Chapter 3

We arrived at the prison.

I hoped my blush had faded.

Rosa's had. So hopefully mine had too.

The three of us went in to see Rico.

He looked awful. As if he hadn't slept at all.

"I need to ask you more questions," Rosa said. "Are you up for it?"

"What else am I going to do?" Rico said.

He wasn't being a wise aleck. He was just tired.

Rosa tried to smile at him.

He tried to smile back.

They were both upset. And doing a bad job at trying to hide it.

"Why did you run from the policeman?" Rosa

asked him.

"I'm late on my payments. For my bike. I'm almost three months behind."

"So?" Rosa asked.

"So I have a friend. He's got a bike, too. His payments were three months behind. And they're trying to repossess his bike. You should *hear* the stories he's been telling me. They'll go to *any* lengths to get his bike."

"So what does that have to do with you?" Rosa asked.

"I thought my bike was being repossessed."

That shocked me.

"You mean, you didn't *know* it was a cop?" I asked.

"No," Rico said. "It was an unmarked car. A pickup truck."

I looked at the public defender.

"Are there unmarked pickup trucks on the force?"

She nodded. "Yes."

"So *that's* why you were evading the police?"

Bloody Knife

Rosa asked.

"I thought it was some crazy re-po guy," he replied.

"The report also said Rico was agitated," Rosa said to the boy's lawyer.

"Is that why you were agitated?" I asked Rico.

"Well, yeah. Wouldn't *you* be? I could make those payments. I was about to pay for a whole month. Then I'd only be two months behind. And it would be paid off. Fully. I wasn't going to let them take my motorcycle because I was late on two payments! Not when I was so close to being paid off!"

"Why were you late on your payments?" his lawyer asked him.

"My mom had some medical bills. I helped her pay them. So I got a little behind. But I had the money now. And I was going to pay!"

I thought back to what Rosa told me about the police report.

The re-po thing explained the evading police and the agitated part.

There was one more thing in that original report.

"What about resisting arrest?" I asked Rico.

"I don't understand why I was arrested to begin with. I hadn't done anything wrong! The guy was tailing me. I tried to ditch him. Next thing I know? I'm getting arrested. Right by the 7-11, on 8th."

I looked at Rosa.

She looked at Rico's lawyer.

"Maybe the guy was ticked off because I made him chase me," Rico said. "I don't know. I don't know why *any* of this is happening!"

"And what about the blood on your helmet?" Rosa asked.

"I don't know anything about that."

"And the bloody rag found in your garage?"

"No clue," he said. "Like I keep *telling* you. I'm being framed."

Rosa looked at me. "We need to keep digging into this."

"Whatever you need," I said. "I'll help any way I can."

Bloody Knife

We left the prison after that.

The lawyer went back to her office.

Rosa and I went to speak with Willie.

We told him what Rico said.

"He could be lying," Willie said.

"He could be telling the truth," Rosa countered.

We looked at that file again.

Rosa wrote down the name of the arresting officer.

"What do you know about him?" Rosa asked Willie.

Willie shrugged.

"Not much. He's new."

Rosa laughed.

"Anyone who's not there twenty *years* is 'new' in your opinion."

Willie laughed. "So?"

"So, how new is new?" Rosa asked.

"Less than a year."

"Where did he come from?"

Willie shrugged. "Beats me. He transferred here."

Chapter 4

Rosa and I were driving back to the junkyard.

"You don't think that's odd?" she asked me.

"What?"

"That this new guy comes to town? Then there's a big rash of murders? And Rico gets framed for murder? Right after he's been pulled over? By the *same* officer who is *new*?"

"It *does* sound hinky," I said.

Rosa giggled.

"What's so funny?" I asked.

"You don't seem like the type to use that word."

"What word?"

"Hinky," she said.

Bloody Knife

"Well, I did."

She smiled. "Yes you did."

"You think Deputy Lawrence has something to do with all this?"

"He might," Rosa said. "I just want to look under every rock. So to speak."

I nodded.

"Do you think Judge Simpkins will know about him?" I asked Rosa.

"He might."

"When we get to the yard, we can call him."

"Okay," she said. "It's worth a shot. I'm getting desperate."

We called as soon as we got there.

"Hi, Judge," I said.

"Hi, Dan. Good to hear from you."

"Rosa's here," I told him.

"Oh. Wonderful. How is she?"

"Not so good. A friend of hers is in trouble. A boy. Rico Vega."

"What kind of trouble are we talking about, son?"

"He was pulled over for speeding. On his motorcycle. By an unmarked car. A pickup truck, really. It turns out he thought he was being followed by a re-po guy."

Judge Simpkins laughed.

"That doesn't sound so bad, Dan. If he's never been in trouble before? It can probably be tossed. Tell Rosa not to worry too much about it."

"Well, it seems his helmet was covered with blood," I explained.

"Oh," he said. "That changes things."

"Yes," I said. "And a bloody rag turned up in his garage when they did a search of his house. Well, his mother's house. The boy lives at home. With his mother."

"Let me guess. A murder victim's blood?"

"That's right," I said. "But the boy *insists* that he didn't do anything!"

"Hm. Let me call my friend and see if he knows anything about this. He usually knows what's going on. And if not? He can find out pretty quickly."

Bloody Knife

"Okay, Judge. Thanks."

"I'll get back to you, Dan."

I hung up the phone.

"He said that he will call a friend. This guy knows everything! He always seems to know what's going on," I told Rosa.

Just then Bubba walked in.

"Unlike me," he said. "What's up? I have no *idea* what's going on."

That made me laugh. "Not only do you *not* know what's going on. But Bubba? You wouldn't know what to *do* about it if you *did*."

Bubba grinned.

"Truer words were probably never spoken," he said.

He plopped down on the couch.

He patted the couch so Lucky would come next to him.

"Come here, Lucky," Bubba called.

Lucky lifted his head.

He looked at Bubba.

Then he got up.

"Hey," Bubba said. "Look at that. I think he's starting to *like* me!"

Then Lucky turned a sharp turn.

Then he jumped onto the loveseat. The loveseat in which Rosa was sitting.

Lucky put his head on her lap.

"Dissed by a dog. That's pretty low," Rosa said to Bubba.

"Hey," Bubba said. "If I had a choice of sitting with me or you? I'd pick you, too!"

The phone rang. It was Judge Simpkins.

I put it on speaker so Rosa could hear.

"Dan? My friend said there's been chatter. In the prisons. There are two guys who *also* swear that they were framed. One is a Jason Atkins. The other is LaMont Jackson. I'll send you their info via email. You should speak with them. The evidence? On all *three* of these cases? It seems too easy. Too perfect. Too cut and dry."

"For Rico's case," I agreed. "It seemed that way to us, too."

"You should probably check it all out."

Bloody Knife

"Do you think this has anything to do with the deputy? The one who pulled Rico over? He's new to the area. Been here only about a year."

"That's when all these murders started," Judge Simpkins said.

"Yes," I said. "We noticed that too."

"What's the deputy's name?"

"Deputy Lawrence," I told him.

"Okay, Dan. I'll see what I can do from this end. But I'll have to be careful. You and Rosa, though, can investigate all you want. Just... be careful. Okay?"

"Okay," I said. "We will. And if your friend finds out anything about this guy? Please pass it along. If you can."

"Will do, son. Will do."

I'd put it on speaker so Rosa could hear. But unfortunately? Bubba heard too.

"That is *so* cool!" Bubba said. "I have no idea what you are talking about. But I want in!"

Chapter 5

Rosa looked at Bubba.

"Let us get started on this," Rosa told him. "And then maybe after, you can help."

Bubba seemed shocked. Like he'd expected Rosa to say no right away.

To tell you the truth? I was shocked too.

Rosa used my computer to get the email from Judge Simpkins. It had all the info we needed to find these two men.

"Let's go here first," Rosa said. She was pointing to LaMont Jackson's prison address. "It's in the next county. It's about an hour away."

"Can I come?" Bubba asked.

"It's best if we keep you out of the loop for

now. So you're not swayed. In case we need you for more important stuff later on," Rosa said.

It sounded like the brush off to *me*. But Bubba was quite impressed with that.

"Okay, Rosa," he replied. "Let me know when you need me."

Rosa and I got in the car and drove.

"What you said to Bubba? That was good," I said.

"I meant it."

My eyes bugged out. "You *did*?"

"Yes. We might need him," she said.

Who was I to argue?! This was *her* thing.

We got to the prison. LaMont was eager to talk to us. He said he'd tell *anyone* he was innocent.

We took a picture of Deputy Lawrence.

"Was this your arresting officer?" we asked.

He barely looked at the picture.

"No. He's white. I got arrested by a brother."

That kind of threw us off. We were hoping this would be an open and shut case.

"Tell us what happened," Rosa said.

"I have no *idea* what happened. I got framed. That's all I know."

"You need to give us more than that. *If* you want us to follow up on it," Rosa said.

"Look. All I know is that I was at work. Bright and early. Next thing I know? A bunch of cops come in and arrest me. They said I murdered this lady."

"What lady?"

"A customer. Some lady from the day before. They said they knew it was me because I was the last person to see her. They said my service ticket was right on her counter."

"Okay. Wait a minute. Step back," Rosa said. "A service ticket for what?"

"I fix air conditioners. In peoples' homes. She was my last stop. She was a nice young lady. She gave me soda. I fixed her air conditioner. Then I left! I didn't kill her. I swear! She was alive."

"Then what happened?"

"The police searched my work van. They said they found a bloody screwdriver in it. I saw it at

Bloody Knife

the trial. It wasn't even my screwdriver!"

"Did you say that at the trial?" Rosa asked.

"Of *course* I did!" he said loudly.

Rosa showed him the picture again.

"Are you *sure* you don't know this man?"

This time he looked at it. "Hey," he said. "Wait a minute. I *do* know this guy. He's a *cop*?!"

"A deputy," I said. "How do you know him?"

"Oh man. That's so weird. It was about a week before all this happened! Dang, it's like from a year ago. But *that's* the dude! I'm *sure* of it."

"What dude?" Rosa asked.

"I'm in my van. Going to the next house. I'm at a light. At the corner of 1st and Davies. Right in front of Burger Prince. And this guy in a big U-Haul truck let's his truck roll back into my van! I went nuts. It was the third time in three months that someone hit my van! My boss said the next time he had to repair my van? He was going to fire me. I didn't want to get fired. So I was *really* ticked off. None of the accidents were my fault! But *I* was going to get fired? It wasn't fair!"

"And *this* was the guy in the U-Haul?" I asked.

"Sure was."

Rosa looked at me. "We have a connection."

"Was *he* the one who framed me? 'Cause if he was? I'm going to kill him!"

"Talk like that won't help you, LaMont," Rosa said to him softly. "Let me see what I can do."

"You believe me?" LaMont asked.

"We will check things out," Rosa said. "I don't know what we'll find. But we'll try. I promise."

That seemed to calm him. "Thanks."

We left there soon after.

"Let's go to the Burger Prince. The one on 1st and Davies. It was a year ago, but maybe someone will remember what happened," Rosa said.

As fate would have it? Deputies were there.

Rosa sent me to get a burger, fries, an apple pie and a milkshake. I got two of each. Except, for the milkshakes? I got one chocolate and one vanilla.

When I got back to the table? Rosa was laughing with the police officers.

"You remember when we were here about a

Bloody Knife

year ago?" she asked me.

I stared at her. I didn't *know* her a year ago!

"Well, wouldn't you know it? It's such a small world! These guys remember it, too. Remember, honey? The guy in the U-Haul rolled into the guy with the van? It was some kind of working place. A plumber or something," Rosa said.

"It was an air conditioning van. And boy was *that* guy mad. He was screaming and yelling. And the guy in the U-Haul? He was just taking it. He just kept saying he was sorry. While the guy in the van ripped him a new one," one deputy said.

He was hooting with laughter.

"Hey. You forgot the funniest part!" his partner said. "Remember the next day? We go into work for roll call? And the sheriff introduced a new deputy? It was Lawrence. And *he* was the guy who got ripped a new one the day before."

"Oh yeah! I remember that," the first guy said. "We ribbed him about that for at least six months! That *was* a long time ago. You're right," he said to Rosa. "Like a year ago."

Chapter 6

We were on our way home.

"So," Rosa said. "It looks like the deputy had a bone to pick with LaMont. LaMont made him look bad in front of his new coworkers. And next thing you know? LaMont is framed for murder."

"And Rico gets pulled over by the deputy. And next thing you know? *Rico* is framed for murder," I noted.

"I'd love to hear what the third inmate says."

"Where is he?" I asked Rosa.

She read off the name of the prison.

"How far away is that?" I asked.

"Too far to visit today. We can go tomorrow."

I looked over at Rosa.

Bloody Knife

"Hopefully? We might have our man," I said.

Rosa sighed loudly.

"That would be great! Now, all we need is some proof," she said.

I nodded.

We got back to the yard. Everything was quiet.

There was a note from Bubba.

Someone bought some parts.

There was also a receipt on my desk. A tow truck brought in a new car.

I'll handle that tomorrow.

Rosa and I sat on the couch.

We turned on the TV.

We were watching CSI.

The sun was shining in my face. It woke me up.

Rosa was nestled in my arms.

We must have fallen asleep. On the couch.

While we watched TV.

I tried not to wake her.

I just stayed there. As still as can be.

It felt good to wake up next to someone again.

It had been a long time.

I looked at Rosa. She was sleeping soundly.

Her dark hair lay across my arm.

She looked beautiful. So calm. And at peace. Like she didn't have a worry in the world.

I knew that wasn't true. She was very worried about Rico.

But while she slept? She was at peace.

She slept for about a half hour longer. Then she woke up.

She looked at me and grinned.

"Hi," she said.

"Good morning," I said.

"I can't believe I fell asleep."

I smiled. "We both did."

She got up and stretched. "Wow, I slept well."

I just realized. I'd slept well too. "Me too."

She rubbed her eyes. "So today we meet the next guy."

"Yes," I said. "But let's have breakfast first. I'm starved. How about some French toast?"

"Sounds yummy."

Bloody Knife

"While I cook? Do you want to go back to your house? To shower and change?"

"That sounds like a plan," she said.

So Rosa left. Then I fed the animals.

Then I started cooking.

I made bacon, too.

And for Rosa? Hot chocolate.

When she got back? She was thrilled.

"Ewww. Hot chocolate. Yum."

We ate, and then we did the dishes. Together.

After that, we left.

"I hope today is as easy as yesterday," I said.

"Me too."

Jason Atkins said he would see us. So that was good.

But what he *said*?

Not so good.

He did not know Deputy Lawrence.

At all.

"Well," Rosa said. "Since we're here. Do you mind answering a few questions?"

"Not at all."

"Tell us what happened," Rosa said.

"To be honest? I don't really know. About six months ago? I was hanging out at home. All of a sudden? The cops bust down my door. They said that I'd murdered someone. I told them I didn't. They asked me where I was three nights before. I told them I was home alone. Watching TV."

"That's it?" Rosa asked.

"That's it."

"You have nothing else to add?" I asked.

"I'm sitting at the trial. Then the police bring out a trophy from my house. It was my high school baseball trophy."

"Why did they bring it out?" I asked.

"They said they found it at the murder scene. But I wasn't anywhere near there! It didn't help that the girl was beaten with a baseball bat. But I swear. I didn't even *know* her. I was at home!"

"Is that why you say you were framed?" Rosa asked.

"No," he said with attitude. "That's how I *was* framed!"

Chapter 7

We were back in the car.

"I'm not seeing a link," Rosa said.

"Me neither."

"We could check out Jason some more. Go deeper. See if anything pops up."

"That's a good idea," I said.

"I'll call Willie. Maybe he can get us some more info."

Willie was out on a call. So Rosa left a message.

We were halfway back to Peaceville.

No one was on the road.

"I want eyes on this guy," Rosa said.

"What?" I asked.

"Deputy Lawrence," she said. "I don't trust him. I want to watch him."

Rosa took out her phone again.

She dialed.

"Bubba?" She said.

"Hey, gorgeous," I heard him reply.

"Remember those night vision glasses you had? At the zoo?"

"The ones you said were ridiculous?" he asked.

I had to speak.

"It was *daytime*! You *did* look ridiculous!"

Rosa waved me off.

"Can I borrow them?" Rosa asked.

"Only if I can come," Bubba said.

Rosa rolled her eyes.

"Okay, Bubba."

Bubba got excited. "I can come?"

"If it's the only way I can get those goggles."

"Oh. Right. Yeah. That's the only way," he said. "I'll be right over. Are you at Dan's place?"

Rosa laughed.

"We're not there yet. We're on our way back

Bloody Knife

from the prison."

"It's okay," he said. "I'll wait for you."

Rosa said goodbye.

I had to laugh.

"What's so funny?" she asked.

"I think you just made a monster."

Rosa laughed too.

"He'll be fine," she said.

"Are you sure, *Law Crusher*?"

Rosa laughed again.

"Those code names *were* funny," she said. "I thought Bubba's was the funniest."

"*Dragon Hunter*?"

Rosa laughed again. "Can you imagine Bubba? Trying to hunt down a dragon?"

I laughed. "The dragon would be safe."

"But Bubba? He'd probably stab himself in the foot," Rosa said.

"Or slice off his own hand," I added.

Rosa giggled.

"That sounds about right," she said.

Rosa's phone rang.

It was Willie.

"Can you do me a favor?" she asked him. "Can you look up a guy named Jason Atkins? I want to know if he has a record."

"Sure," he said. "Hang on."

Rosa turned to me.

"Both Rico and LaMont were clean. Neither had a record. But Jason? He seemed different."

I heard Willie speak.

"You're right on target," Willie said.

"He has a sheet?" she asked.

"He has a long one. But it's mostly minor stuff. Petty theft, burglary and attempted burglary, to name a few. No violence, though. His murder was the first time he got violent."

"You don't think that's weird?" Rosa asked.

"I don't know. Stuff like that happens," he said.

"How many attempted burglaries?"

"Two."

"What happened?" Rosa asked.

"Hang on. Let me look them up."

Rosa put her hand over the phone.

Bloody Knife

"This might tell us something," she told me.

"Like what?" I asked.

She shrugged. "Could be anything."

I heard Willie.

"One, they couldn't pin on him. Not enough evidence. For the second one? The people came home. And he left. But they didn't press charges."

"And he didn't beat them with a baseball bat?"

"No," Willie said.

"And he didn't leave his baseball trophy behind? At the scene?" Rosa asked.

"No."

Rosa looked at me and winked.

"And you don't think it's, ah, *hinky* that he brought his trophy to a *murder*? And then *left* it there?!"

"That is a little clean. Isn't it," Willie mumbled.

"Yes. It's a little too easy. If you'd ask me," Rosa said.

She told Willie all about LaMont.

"That's a little too clean and easy, too," Willie noted.

"Yes," Rosa said. "I agree."

"But there's no link," I reminded Rosa. "Nothing that links Lawrence and Jason."

"My gut says? There *has* to be," Rosa said.

"Want to look through Jason Atkins's file yourself?" Willie offered.

"I'd love to," Rosa replied.

"We can swing by there now," I told Rosa.

"Great," she said. "We'll see you soon, Willie."

"Okay. Just don't tell anyone I let you do this."

"I won't," Rosa assured him.

We got there in ten minutes.

Rosa looked through the records.

"These are all thefts. No violence. All stuff you can easily pawn. Jason was a lazy thief. No heavy lifting. If it didn't fit in his pocket? He left it," Rosa said.

"Did you read about the art collector?" Willie asked. "That was funny."

I looked at Rosa.

"Jason robbed an art collector. The art was

Bloody Knife

worth *millions*."

"What did Jason get?" I asked.

Rosa read through the report.

Then she laughed.

"He took some gold jewelry. And a couple of small pieces. Gifts from the owner's grandchild."

"Why is that funny?" I asked.

"The gifts? They were from the dollar store."

I laughed. "That *is* funny."

"What's funnier is that our boy Jason? He left four Fabergé eggs," Rosa read aloud.

"They can be expensive," I said.

"You're not kidding," Rosa said. "One of the eggs? It was worth five and a half *million* dollars."

"And that's just *one* of the eggs," Willie said.

"So Jason is basically a criminal," I noted.

"And a very *stupid* criminal," Willie said.

Rosa giggled. "So. It seems that the bottom line of this whole thing is that our Jason Atkins is just... um... criminally stupid."

Chapter 8

Bubba was at the yard.

"Where *were* you guys?" he asked.

"We stopped at the police station."

I saw an empty bag of chips.

It was next to the chair.

The chair that faced the TV.

I saw an empty pretzel bag, too.

"Did you eat *everything*?" I asked Bubba.

Bubba shrugged.

"I had nothing else to do."

I threw out the bags. And the empty soda cans.

"Do you have the goggles?" Rosa asked.

"Right here," Bubba said.

He took them from his backpack.

Bloody Knife

"I have Lawrence's home address. I want to follow him," Rosa said.

"You said I could come," Bubba said.

Rosa nodded.

"You can come, Bubba. But you have to stay low. And keep quiet."

"I can do that," he said.

"Too bad you don't do it more often," I said.

Rosa laughed.

"Say what you will," Bubba said. "I know you love me."

I rolled my eyes.

"Are you guys ready?" Rosa asked.

"For what?" Bubba asked.

Rosa took a deep breath.

"To watch the *deputy*."

"Shouldn't we stop for food?" Bubba asked.

"You ate half the food in my house!" I roared. "How can you be hungry?!"

"I just am!" Bubba said. "Do you mind?"

"We'll get food on the way," Rosa said. "Now whose car should we use?"

"We can take the red Mustang," Bubba said.

"No. That stands out too much," Rosa said.

"I thought you sold that?" I asked Bubba.

"I did. He's not coming till tomorrow to get it."

"So you want to use it in a stakeout *today*?!" I said.

"Why not?" Bubba asked.

"What if we get shot at? Did you tell the guy it has bullet holes in it?"

"Oh," Bubba said. "Good point."

"So whose car should we use?" I asked Rosa.

"Your car is too small," she said to me.

"I have an old La Baron. It's dark blue," Bubba offered.

"That sounds good. Okay. We'll use that," Rosa said.

We took the red Mustang to Bubba's shop.

We traded it for the dark blue car.

"Yes," Rosa said. "This'll work."

We stopped at the food mart and got snacks.

Rosa bought lots of chocolate treats.

I got some salty snacks.

Bloody Knife

And Bubba got anything he could get his hands on.

Of course, I paid.

We got to the address Rosa had.

We waited for the deputy to come home.

It was a long wait.

He finally showed up.

That's when Bubba seemed to wake up.

"I'm starved," he said. "Can you hand me something to eat?"

The sun had set by then. Rosa had the night vision goggles on.

"I'm a little busy right now, Bubba," she said.

"Sniper Buddy? Can you please pass me some food?"

"Stop calling me Sniper Buddy," I said.

"Hey," Bubba said. "I said 'please.'"

God, he was annoying!

"All right. What do you want?" I asked.

"Hand me a frozen burrito, please."

"A *frozen burrito*?!" I roared.

"Shhhh," Rosa said. "We don't want anyone to

know we're here."

"Sorry," I whispered to Rosa.

I turned to Bubba.

"A frozen burrito? For *real*?! How are you going to heat it up?!"

"By now? I'd have to say it's partly thawed. I'll eat it like that."

I looked through the bag of food.

And there it was. A frozen burrito.

He also got a frozen pizza.

"A *frozen pizza*?" I whispered as loudly as I could. "What kind of idiot gets a frozen pizza for a stakeout?!"

Bubba didn't take offense.

"A hungry idiot," was his reply.

I threw his burrito at him.

"Just sit and eat," I told Bubba. "And don't talk. Okay?"

"Whatever you say, Sniper Buddy."

I tried to ignore him.

But it was hard.

"You make a lot of noise when you eat," I

Bloody Knife

muttered to Bubba.

"It's hard to believe. But these are *good* when they're frozen."

I pictured myself taking a frozen burrito. And carving it to a point. Then jamming it into my eye.

It would be less painful than putting up with all of this.

If it were just Rosa and me?

That would have been nice.

And fun.

But having Bubba along?

Not nice. And not fun.

Every minute felt like an hour.

Things were slow.

I thought I'd try to start a chat.

"So where'd you get *this* car?" I asked Bubba.

"Someone dropped it off for an oil change."

"It's a *customer's* car?!" I roared.

"Shhhh," Rosa said.

"Who takes a customer's car on a stakeout?!" I whispered loudly.

Bubba grinned. "We do."

Chapter 9

Deputy Lawrence was in his house.

"I need to get close," Rosa said. "I want to see what he's doing."

"I'm going with you," I said.

"I want to come too," Bubba said.

"No, Bubba," Rosa said. "You stay here."

"How come?!" he whined.

"In case he takes off. We need someone in the car to get us."

Bubba didn't look pleased.

Rosa strapped on the goggles.

"Well... if you fall and break both your legs? Don't come running to me!" he said to Rosa.

Rosa laughed.

Bloody Knife

"That's funny," she said.

Bubba folded his arms across his chest.

"It wasn't supposed to be," he muttered.

Rosa softened.

"Bubba. I really *do* need someone in the car. To follow him in case he takes off."

"Why can't *Dan* stay in the car?" he whined.

"Because you're the better mechanic. What if the car stalls? *You're* the best man for the job."

Bubba made a face.

"Yeah. I guess you're right," he said.

So Rosa and I took off.

We snuck around the side of the house.

We looked in the deputy's windows.

He was sitting at his computer.

"Can you see what he's doing?" Rosa whispered to me.

"No. Can you?"

"No. The screen is facing the wrong way."

Just then, he got up.

He walked out of the room.

Rosa went one way. I went the other way.

He didn't go my way. So I walked over to Rosa.

"You have him?" I asked.

"Yes," she whispered.

"What's he doing?" I asked.

"Looks like he's getting ready to go out."

I peeked inside. At the window next to Rosa's.

He was grabbing his keys.

Putting money in his wallet.

Slipping his wallet into his back pocket.

He took a jacket from his closet.

He slipped it on.

He sprayed on some cologne.

He sniffed his right armpit area.

He grabbed some mints.

"Oh yes," I whispered to Rosa. "He's going out. Most likely with a girl."

Rosa winked at me.

"Is that what you do?"

I shook my head.

"I don't sniff my armpits."

Rosa smiled.

Bloody Knife

"I'm glad to hear that," she said.

The deputy left his house. He got in his car.

We hid behind the bushes.

Bubba pulled up to get us.

We got in the car.

"Hey," he said. "You were right, Rosa. You needed me."

"See?" she said.

Bubba followed the deputy's car.

He met someone at a restaurant.

We had to sit and wait for them to come out.

It took two hours.

Two hours with Bubba.

When we got there? We had changed seats. I got in the driver's seat. Bubba got in the back. (With the bag of food.)

After about an hour and a half? Rosa turned to me.

"You're a saint," she said.

I had to smile.

"No I'm not," I told her.

She threw her gaze at Bubba.

He was now eating his frozen pizza. Unfrozen. And raw.

"Yes you are," she said.

I shook my head.

"I would have killed him long ago. But *you're* here."

She laughed.

"I *heard* that," Bubba said.

Rosa and I laughed.

We sat and waited some more.

And we listened to Bubba eat.

But mostly, we were silent.

I reached over and took Rosa's hand.

I hoped Bubba didn't notice.

But we were in the dark.

So I figured he wouldn't see.

We'd been sitting like that for half an hour.

Holding hands.

It was nice. *Really* nice.

I think we were *both* trying to ignore Bubba.

At least I know *I* was.

"I'm feeling queasy," Bubba said.

Chapter 10

"Maybe you shouldn't have eaten so much," Rosa offered.

"Or it might be that raw pizza," I threw in.

"I have a belly ache," he said.

I looked at Rosa.

I smirked.

"It's like having kids," I said.

"Our own oversized baby," she said. "Right in the back seat."

"Would you two knock it off?!" Bubba said. "I feel like I'm going to hurl."

I saw the deputy leaving the restaurant.

He had a girl on his arm.

I wondered if he was going to murder her.

Rosa saw it too.

"You'd better hold it in, Bubba," she said. "Because we have to roll."

I started the car.

I waited for them to pull out of the parking lot.

"Okay go," Rosa said.

I swung out and got behind them.

"Don't get too close," Rosa said. "We want him to do what he is going to do."

"What's he going to do?" Bubba asked.

"I don't know," Rosa said. "But I don't want to spook him."

We followed him to a house.

The girl got out her keys.

She opened the door.

They both went in.

Rosa opened the car door.

"I want to see what's happening in there."

I grabbed her arm.

"You're not going without me," I told her.

"Okay," she whispered.

"I'm coming too," Bubba said.

Bloody Knife

"Oh no you're not," I said.

Bubba looked at Rosa.

"We still need someone in the car. In case he takes off," she said.

"Like after he kills her?" Bubba asked. "That would make my job very important."

"Let's hope that doesn't happen," Rosa said. "But yes. In case that happens."

"No problem, Law Crusher. I'm your man."

We closed the doors. Quietly.

I grabbed Rosa's hand.

"Don't get too close," I said.

"We *have* to, Dan."

She was right.

But I wasn't happy about it.

"Be careful," I said.

She held her finger to her lips.

Then she nodded.

We looked inside a window.

They were sitting on a couch.

Watching TV.

He had his arm around her.

She was snuggled next to him.

They were just watching TV.

Well, *he* was watching TV.

She was reading a book.

Every now and then, she'd look at him.

They'd smile.

Then she would go back to reading.

And he would go back to watching TV.

This was not the scene of a new couple.

These two were together for a while.

I could tell.

They were comfortable together.

Secure in their relationship.

Otherwise, she wouldn't read while he watched TV.

I whispered this to Rosa.

She agreed.

We snuck away from the window.

"I don't think he plans on killing her," Rosa said.

"Me neither," I agreed.

"I wonder who she is," Rosa said.

Bloody Knife

"Maybe her name is on the mailbox."

We walked to the mailbox.

And there it was.

A last name and the street address.

"Wait a minute," Rosa said.

"What's the matter?" I asked.

"This name looks familiar to me. So does the address."

"From where?" I asked her.

She thought about it.

"I need to go to the police station again," she said.

We got to the car.

Bubba had moved to the driver's side.

Rosa got in the car.

"We need to go to the police station," she told Bubba.

"Can you drive?" Bubba asked me. "I still don't feel well."

I got behind the wheel.

Bubba got in the back.

We drove to the station.

Chapter 11

"Oh my goodness," Rosa said. "I was right."

"About what?" Willie asked.

"Her name and address," she said.

"Who is she?" I asked Rosa.

"One of Jason's victims."

Willie laughed.

"What did he do? Steal her fake jewelry and spare change?" Willie asked.

Rosa and I looked at Willie.

I forgot. He wasn't in the loop.

"We just got back from following the deputy," I told Willie.

"Where did he go?" Willie asked.

"To what appears to be his girlfriend's house."

Bloody Knife

"So? The man has a girlfriend. That's not a crime," Willie said.

"Remember there was one robbery they couldn't pin on Jason? So he walked?"

Willie nodded. "Yeah. So?"

"So. The victim? She's the deputy's girlfriend."

"Hm," Willie said. "Now *that's* not good."

"Add LaMont's accident with Lawrence? And Rico's arrest? And all three killers are connected. To Deputy Lawrence."

Willie groaned.

"Oh, no. This is not good," he said. "Not good at all!"

He shook his head.

"Are you sure that's the woman?" Willie asked.

"She's right in the police report."

"Who wrote the police report?" Willie asked.

"Another deputy."

"Was Lawrence on the scene for that case?"

"No," Rosa said.

"And *that* was the case that they didn't have proof?"

"Yes," Rosa replied.

"So they couldn't pin it on Jason Atkins?" he asked.

"That's correct," Rosa said.

"And they had to let Atkins walk?" he asked.

"Yes," Rosa confirmed.

Willie shook his head.

"This is *not* good at all!" he said softly.

"Look," Rosa said. "We have nothing concrete yet. Let us keep looking into this."

"If this gets out? We're in trouble," Willie said.

"Why would *you* be in trouble?" I asked.

"Not me. The entire sheriff's office."

"Why?" I asked him.

He looked at me.

"Every arrest he made will get repealed. Any case he was *involved* with... will get messed up."

"That *is* bad," I said.

"So let us keep looking into it," Rosa said.

Willie nodded slowly.

"That probably would be best."

Chapter 12

Bubba was in the back seat.
Sleeping.
He was snoring like a bear.
"Should we wake him?" Rosa asked.
I rolled my eyes.
"It's so much easier when he's asleep."
Rosa giggled softly.
"Okay. Let's just let him sleep."
We drove back to the girl's house.
We snuck back up to the window.
"They're still inside," Rosa said.
I nodded.
He was still watching TV.
She was still reading.

Elise Leonard

They were both still alive.

I guess that was a good thing.

"So what now?" I asked Rosa.

"We watch him."

"For what?"

She shrugged.

"Who knows?"

Nothing much happened after that.

It got late. It was time for him to go.

He kissed her goodbye.

He left.

We followed him home.

So we went home, too.

But first? We had to drop off Bubba.

"Bubba, you're back home," Rosa said.

Bubba woke up. Then he looked around.

"Well *that* was a waste of time," he said.

"Not really," Rosa said.

"What did I miss?" Bubba asked.

I didn't want to explain it to Bubba.

Neither did Rosa.

"You're right," I told him. "You didn't miss

Bloody Knife

anything."

"Do you feel okay?" Rosa asked Bubba.

Bubba nodded.

"No problem. I'm fine now."

I looked at Rosa.

"And he didn't even have to get his stomach pumped."

"It's a miracle," Rosa said.

We left and went back to the yard.

Rosa came in for a while.

We sat around and talked.

Mostly about the case.

Rosa was excited. She was getting close.

She was hoping to get Rico freed.

"So you think the deputy framed Rico?" I asked her.

"It's sure looking that way."

It was.

"But I still want proof," she said. "So can we go there again tomorrow?"

"Sure," I said.

"I'd like to get there early," she said.

"How early?" I asked.

"Before sunrise. So he won't suspect."

I shrugged. "Sure."

She looked at her watch.

"It's getting late. I'd better go."

She only had a few hours to sleep.

"Would you like to stay here?" I offered. "I can sleep on the couch."

"You don't have to sleep on the couch," she said. "I can sleep on the couch."

I shook my head.

"You take the bed. It's comfortable. I'll take the couch."

It was her turn to shake her head.

"You're too big for the couch. I slept very well last night. I'll take the couch," she said.

We really didn't need to have had that chat.

Turns out? We were watching TV again.

And we both fell asleep on the couch. Again.

When we woke up? She said, "I could get used to this."

So could I.

Chapter 13

We washed up quickly.

I made breakfast.

Just cereal. We were pressed for time.

It was a good thing we got there early.

The deputy was already leaving his house.

"Where's *he* off to this early?" I said aloud.

"Follow him," Rosa said.

We did.

He drove to the water.

He got in a boat.

He took off.

"What do you think he's up to?" Rosa asked.

"Who knows?" I said.

"He's probably burying a body," Bubba said at

Rosa's window.

Rosa jumped.

She let out a little yelp.

"You scared me to death!" she told him.

Bubba laughed.

"See? You guys think I'm not a good spy. I'm a *great* spy!"

"You were spying on *us*?" I asked him.

He waved me off.

"Nah," he said. "I got up early. To detail the Mustang. For the guy who's buying it."

"So how did you get *here*?"

"I took it for one last spin. And I saw you pass by."

"Well," Rosa said. "We're still watching the deputy. But we lost him."

"He went out on a boat," I explained.

Bubba looked out at the water.

He pointed.

"That boat?" he said.

"That's the one," I said.

"Want to follow him?" Bubba asked.

Bloody Knife

"How?"

Bubba shrugged.

"That's easy. I can hot wire any of these boats."

I looked at Rosa.

She looked at me.

"It *is* illegal," I said.

"But I *do* want to know what he's doing," Rosa said.

We turned to Bubba.

"Okay," I said.

"Let's go," Rosa said.

Bubba whooped.

"This is going to be so much fun!"

"It won't hurt the boat. Will it?" Rosa asked.

Bubba grinned.

"Don't worry. I'll leave it in better shape than we found it."

"Well," I said. "We really didn't 'find' it."

"We just... borrowed it," Bubba said.

"But you'll leave it in better shape?" Rosa asked.

"Sure will," Bubba said.

He pointed to the boats at the dock.

"Pick your pleasure," he said.

"Any one?" Rosa asked.

"Any one," Bubba said.

She picked one that looked like it hadn't been used for a while.

"You picked the worst-looking one!" Bubba said.

"I'm hoping the owners won't come while we have it out," she replied.

"I would have picked that one," Bubba said.

He pointed to the biggest boat on the dock.

"It's a little gaudy. Isn't it?" I asked.

"If you're going to go out?" Bubba said. "You might as well go out in style."

"This one will do," Rosa said.

We waited while Bubba got it started.

It started right up.

It spluttered and coughed a little.

Bubba went to the engines.

He fiddled around a little.

They started to purr.

Bloody Knife

"You see?" Bubba said. "We'll return it better than we got it."

"Okay," Rosa said.

She pointed to the little boat in the distance.

"Can you catch up to him?"

Bubba grinned.

"Hang on to her, Sniper Buddy!" he said to me.

And then he took off.

It was a good thing he'd warned me.

Because if I hadn't been holding on to Rosa? She would have flown off the back of the boat.

It was actually a good time.

Rosa's hair was whipping in the wind.

Her cheeks were flushed.

Bubba was making our boat fly.

I could tell he was having fun.

Rosa was having fun, too.

And me? I was having a blast.

Enjoying every moment.

Even if we *were* chasing a killer. In a stolen boat.

Chapter 14

The only problem?

He didn't *do* anything.

Not that we could tell, at least.

He just took his boat out for a ride.

That was it.

We didn't see him bring any bodies.

We didn't see him dump any bodies.

There were no bodies.

Just his.

And he looked like he just went for a ride on his boat.

Which, I must say.

Was a blast.

I'd never gone on a boat ride before.

Bloody Knife

Well. Not like this.

I've been on a cruise.

I've been on a yacht.

I've been on a large sailboat.

But this?

This was fun.

A *lot* of fun!

I turned to Bubba.

"We should get a boat," I told him.

"Sure, bud. That would be cool."

Rosa laughed at us.

"Boys with their toys."

I had to laugh.

"Oh come on, honey. Admit it. You had fun."

She blushed prettily.

Oh my goodness! I just called her "honey." And in front of *Bubba*!

"Yes," she said. "I had a lot of fun."

Rosa was looking at me.

We were smiling.

"I hate to tell you. But while you guys are making gaga eyes at each other? Your guy is leaving."

"What?!" Rosa said.

"He's tied up his boat. Secured it. And now he's back in his car," Bubba said.

Rosa turned to look at him.

"He's probably going to work now," she said.

Bubba tied up our boat.

He secured it, too.

"You should probably leave a little money for gas, Dan. We used up a bit."

"Where should I leave it?"

Bubba showed me a good place to hide it.

"They will find it here. But it's not out in the open for anyone to take."

I helped Rosa off the boat.

She wobbled a little. Then she fell into my arms.

"I've got you," I said softly.

She looked up at me.

"Yes, you do," she said quietly.

Bubba laughed at Rosa.

"What's the matter? Don't have your land legs

Bloody Knife

yet?"

"We should follow him," I said.

"He's probably just going to work," Rosa said.

"He's getting away," Bubba said.

"Let him," she replied. "We have other things to do."

"Like what?" I asked.

"Like check out his boat," she answered.

"Good thinking," Bubba said. "We should search his boat."

People started coming to the dock.

It was starting to get crowded.

"We need a lookout," Rosa said.

"*I* can do that," Bubba said.

Rosa grinned.

"It's a good thing you showed up," she said.

"Yeah," Bubba said. "To be the lookout."

I rolled my eyes.

"Oh yes," I said aloud. "It's a good thing."

Rosa cracked up.

Chapter 15

"Did you find anything?" Bubba asked.

"Nothing," I said.

"That boat was clean," Rosa said.

"Too clean?" Bubba asked.

"No," Rosa said. "Just normal clean. Like a guy with a boat. Who takes care of it."

"Nothing weird," I added.

"Bummer," Bubba said.

"I know," Rosa said.

"It would have been so much easier if we found something," I stated.

"You're sure?" Bubba asked.

Rosa nodded.

"There's nothing on that boat that doesn't

belong."

"Well," Bubba said. "I have to get back to the shop. My buyer will come soon."

"Say goodbye to the Mustang from me," I said.

Bubba grimaced.

"I will."

"You're going to miss her. Huh?" Rosa asked.

Bubba nodded.

He took off.

Rosa and I stayed by the water for a little while longer.

We walked hand in hand.

"That was fun," I said.

She smiled. "Yes, it was."

"This life? Living in Florida? It's so much different than my life in New York."

"Is it better?" she asked.

"Oh, yes. Much!"

"You *should* get a boat," Rosa said.

"And if I get it with Bubba? He can take care of it. Mechanically."

Rosa smiled widely.

"Sounds like a plan."

I stopped walking.

Since we were holding hands? Rosa had to stop too.

"Rosa?"

"Yes?"

"I know you're just on vacation. But do you think you'll ever want to move back here?" I asked.

I can't believe I came out and asked her that.

I mean, I really didn't have any right to ask.

I was still married. To Patti.

And Rosa had a job. A life. Out of state.

She had no job here.

Sure. She had friends.

And a house.

But no job. No security. No protection.

She looked at me and smiled warmly.

"I'd *love* to move back home. But I don't have a job here."

I knew she'd say that.

But I was glad to hear that she wanted to come

Bloody Knife

back to Peaceville.

For now? That was good enough.

I could still be hopeful.

We drove back to the yard.

I had to feed the animals. I also had work to do.

So Rosa called Mel.

Mel didn't have a photo shoot. So she stopped by.

I could hear the girls laughing and giggling.

They were having a blast.

I have no idea what they were talking about.

But they sure were having fun.

It felt good to be working. And all the while, hearing laughter in the background.

That's how work should be for everyone.

It sure wasn't how work was on Wall Street.

And I'd bet it wasn't how work was at Rosa's law firm.

But in my new life? Work could be that way.

Life was good.

I was in my office when I heard Rosa's phone

ring.

She started yelling.

First she yelled, "You're kidding!"

Then she listened some more.

Then she yelled, "No way!"

I ran into the living room.

Mel and Rosa were sitting on the couch.

"What's going on?" I asked Mel.

"I have no idea!" Mel said.

I watched Rosa.

She listened to the person on the phone some more.

"Look," she said. "This can't be!"

She paused to listen to the caller.

"When?" she asked.

She listened to the answer.

"There's no way!" she said again.

She looked up at me.

Her eyes showed shock.

"I can't tell you why," she said into the phone. "Just let me get back to you. Okay?!"

She sounded hysterical.

Bloody Knife

She hung up her cell.

"What's wrong?" I asked.

"You're not going to *believe* this!"

"*What*?!" Mel asked.

"The police got a tip. They followed up on it."

"What kind of tip?" I asked.

"They were told to look for a bloody knife. On Deputy Lawrence's boat!"

"*What*?!" I said.

"And the weird thing is? They *followed* the tip. And *found* a bloody *knife*!"

"When?" I asked.

"About a half hour after we were there!"

"That's not possible!" I said.

"Why not?" Mel asked.

"Because *we* searched that boat. And there was nothing there!" Rosa said.

"And we walked around for a half hour after that," I added.

"And got back to Dan's car at that time," Rosa said.

"And the deputy never came back," I said.

"The police must have come *moments* after we left," Rosa said.

"This is insane," I said.

"There *was* no knife on that boat," Rosa said.

"Wow," Mel says. "This whole thing sounds hinky!"

Rosa and I looked at each other.

We grinned.

"It sure does!" we said together.

My mind was racing.

"We're missing something," I said to Rosa.

"Yes," she said. "I agree."

"I want to see that knife," I said.

"Me, too," Rosa said.

"What knife?" Bubba said.

He snuck into my house.

"What are *you* doing here?" I asked him.

"The guy came. He bought my baby. She's gone. And I'm a little bummed."

He looked around.

"What did I miss?" he asked.

"The police got a tip," Rosa said.

Bloody Knife

"A bloody knife on the deputy's boat," I added.

"But you guys searched that boat," he said.

He looked at us.

"And you came up empty. Didn't you?" he asked.

"Yes!" we said together.

"So what's this all about?" he asked.

I shook my head.

So did Rosa.

"I don't know," we said together.

"I want to see that knife," Rosa said.

"So do I," I said.

"Me too," Bubba said.

"Look," I said to Bubba. "We can be in *big* trouble for searching that boat."

"And we can *all* get in big trouble for stealing that *other* boat," he said.

Mel gasped.

"You stole a *boat*?!" she cried out.

"We gave it back," Rosa said.

"In better shape," Bubba added.

"And I left gas money," I said.

Mel laughed.

"You're the worst criminals I ever met."

Rosa looked at me.

"She's obviously never met Jason."

"Who's Jason?" Mel asked.

"He's a killer," Bubba said.

"Who can't tell the difference between a dollar-store nick-nack and a Fabergé egg," I explained.

"What are you people talking about?!" Mel wailed.

"Look," Rosa said. "We have to go. But we'll explain later."

Rosa, Bubba and I flew out of there.

"Where to?" I asked Rosa.

"The police station."

We got there in no time.

Willie was surprised to see us.

"We need to see that knife," Rosa said.

"It's evidence," Willie said.

"We know," Rosa said. "But we need to see it."

"It's in lockup. You *know* I can't show it to you."

Chapter 16

"It's in a bag, right?" Bubba asked.

"Yes? So?"

"So we won't touch it. We just want to *see* it," Bubba pleaded.

Willie looked at Rosa.

"Please?" she begged Willie.

Willie sighed loudly. Then he whispered.

"I guess it's okay. But you can only *look* at it. You can't touch it. *Don't* take it out of the bag."

"We won't," we all agreed.

He took us near the evidence room.

"Wait here," Willie told us.

We waited.

"Do you need a break?" Willie asked the guy.

"Yeah. I could use one," the officer said.

"Go ahead," Willie said. "I'll watch the cage for you."

The guy shrugged. "Gee, thanks, Willie."

"No problem," Willie said.

As soon as the officer left? He snuck us back there.

He looked up the number. Then he found the knife.

"Make it fast," he whispered.

He held the knife out to us.

The bag messed up our view.

We got closer.

"Hey," Bubba said. "That's one of those fancy knives. It's the Buckskin Original Limited Edition Pearl Classic."

We stared at Bubba.

He shrugged.

"I watch a lot of late night TV."

We looked at the knife.

Bubba reached out for the knife.

"Let me see that," Bubba said.

Bloody Knife

Willie reacted.

He pulled the bag away. Quickly.

The bag and the knife went flying.

Right into the steel cage.

It landed on the floor.

Even *I* heard the sound as it shattered.

We ran over to the baggie on the floor.

The bloody knife was still in it.

But the pearl handle? It was shattered.

"Now look what you made me do!" Willie yelled at Bubba.

"Hey," Bubba said. "I didn't even *touch* it."

"You were grabbing at it!" Willie said.

"No I wasn't!" Bubba argued.

Bubba looked at the knife. In the bag. On the floor.

"Hey," Bubba said. "Look! I *told* you it was an original. Under the handle, it says 3702."

"What?" I asked.

"They're all numbered," Bubba said.

"Well, if it has a *number*," Rosa said. "Maybe we can find out who *bought* it."

The guy was coming back. I could hear him humming.

"You'd better get that back to its spot," I said.

Willie picked up the knife. The handle was now broken into tiny pieces. There was no handle left.

"Great," Willie mumbled. "Just great."

We got out of there before the guy came back.

We waited by Willie's desk.

Willie came back a few seconds later.

"If I wasn't soon to retire? I'm sure I'd be fired," he said to us.

"No one will know," Bubba said.

"*I'll* know," Willie said.

"I'm sorry, Willie. But I need to go somewhere. Can you call this Buckskin place? And find out who bought the pearl knife? Number 3702?"

"Sure, Rosa." He looked at Bubba. Then he looked back at Rosa. "I'll do it for *you*."

He thought that would bother Bubba?

He didn't know Bubba.

And speaking of which? Bubba said, "So where are we going?"

Bloody Knife

"To the 7-11 on 8th Avenue," Rosa answered.

"Oh good. I could use a slurpee," Bubba said.

"Why are we going there?" I asked.

We piled into my car.

"Because I want to see if they have any video outside. You know, for safety," she said.

"That's a great idea," I said.

"What is?" Bubba asked.

"Maybe we can see the arrest on video," I said.

"Or catch the deputy smearing blood on Rico's helmet."

"That would be cool," Bubba said. "I was just glad to go get a slurpee."

When we got there? We were happy.

We'd lucked out.

They *did* have video pointed outside.

And it was aiming right where Rico was pulled over.

And... they had tapes from the whole month.

The manager said we could watch. As long as we each bought something.

So we all bought slurpees.

As we sipped, we watched.

We saw Rico and the deputy.

We saw the whole arrest.

"The deputy never touched the helmet," I said.

"Can you see any blood on it?" Rosa asked.

"It's dark," I said. "But I don't see any."

"That stinks," Bubba said. "The deputy never even *touched* the helmet."

Rosa sighed. "Well, between the time he was arrested? And the time it came in the impound lot? The blood appeared."

"The deputy is putting Rico in the car," I said.

"And they're taking off," Bubba said.

We were about to shut off the tape.

There was nothing left to see.

"Wait," Bubba said. "I know that car!"

"What car?" I asked.

Bubba pointed to the tape. "*That* car."

A car had pulled up behind the motorcycle.

The motorcycle that was waiting—all alone—for the impound guys to pick it up.

"That's Sheriff Daley's car. A white Cadillac

Bloody Knife

DeVille," Bubba said. "I've worked on it."

"And there's the sheriff," Rosa said.

"Yup," Bubba said. "That's him."

"Look," I said, "He's taking the helmet off the handlebars."

"He's wiping down the helmet," Bubba said.

"Or putting something *on* it!" I said.

"Oh my *God*!" Rosa screamed.

She took out her phone. She went to dial.

Her phone rang.

She looked at the incoming call.

"It's Willie," she said.

She answered the phone.

"I know who it is!" she said into the phone.

Willie had said the *exact same thing*! At the *exact same time*!

"It's Sheriff Daley!" they both said.

"How did *you* know?" Willie asked.

"He's on video tape, putting blood on Rico's helmet! How did *you* know?" Rosa asked Willie.

"*He* bought the knife!" Willie said.

"We got him!" Rosa said.

"Where's Bubba?" Willie asked. "I could *kiss* that bumbling idiot!"

Bubba grinned. "Don't get all crazy on me, dude. *Nobody* gets a kiss from *these* lips. At least not without buying me *dinner* first!"

"So it turns out? The sheriff was insane," Rosa told Mel.

"He was a heartless killer. Went out of his way to pin his murders on innocent people," I added.

"And if that didn't work? He had a backup fall guy. Deputy Lawrence," Rosa explained.

"He was so arrogant? He kept trinkets. From all his murders! He killed *six* people," Willie said.

"And if it weren't for Rosa? *Six* people would still be in prison. For *life*," I said.

But the best part was? Rosa was *all over* the news. For finding a serial killer. (The *sheriff*!) And all three local counties want her to run for sheriff.

I hope she takes them up on that.

That'll bring her back here. Back home.

To me.

Now that Dan and Rosa (and Bubba)
have solved *this* problem,
please read the next **JUNKYARD DAN** book,
entitled
TAKING NAMES AND KICKING ASSETS,
to find out what's going to happen
with Dan and Rosa.
Will they finally get together?
Now that Rosa has been offered a job,
will she move back home?
Will Patti leave them alone? Will *Bubba*?
Find out by reading the *next* book in the series!

And we have a few **other** series that you might like too:

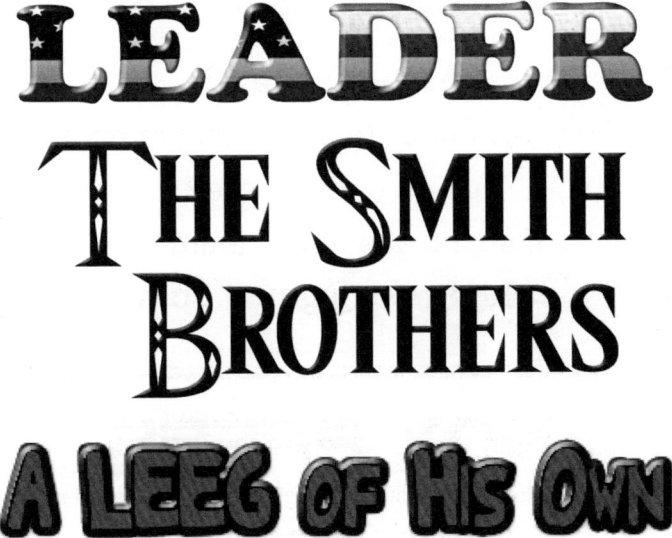

Want to read more NOX PRESS books?

Go online to
www.NoxPress.com
to see what's being released!

Books can easily be purchased online or you can contact **Nox Press** via the Website for quantity discounts.

Are you a fan?

Do you want us to put *your* comments up on our Website?
If so, please e-mail them to:
NoxPress@gmail.com

NOX PRESS
books for that extra kick to give you more power
www.NoxPress.com